DRAGON LAKE

A Swan Lake Retelling

Printed in the United States of America

ISBN 978-1-7351315-1-1 (ebook)

ISBN 978-1-7351315-2-8 (paperback)

Published by Night Muse Press

Cover by Maria Spada Design

Edited by J. E. Feldman

NIGHT MUSE PRESS
EST. 2020

ACKNOWLEDGEMENTS

To Jesse and Jena, who give me wings to fly.
To Bonnie and Taylor, who kept me sane during daylight.
To Kim, who was by my side no matter what.
To my readers, who never cease to amaze
me with their support and generosity.
To Maria, who designed an incredible cover
and was a joy to work with as always.
And to Odette, who taught me that freedom
is worth fighting for.

Also by R. L. Davennor:

Lyres, Legends, and Lullabies: An Annotated Score Collection

Unable are the Loved to die
For Love is Immortality,
Nay, it is Deity—

Unable they that love—to die
For Love reforms Vitality
Into Divinity.

EMILY DICKINSON

DRAGON LAKE

en are foolish, predictable creatures.

This one was no different.

I peered out from the tree concealing me and waited, scanning the moonlit forest for the prince that believed he chased a helpless, innocent maiden.

I was neither.

The dragon within me writhed as she always did at night, clawing and scraping at my insides even harder now that my target was near. He'd fallen behind and wouldn't be able to make out details through the mist.

He wouldn't be able to tell the dragon was me.

I gathered my dress in my fists. Silver embroidery trailed up the sleeves and the garment wasn't cumbersome—a rare find. The minute I shifted, it would be ruined like all the others. If I took it off while still in one piece, I could retrieve it later...and surely I deserved such a luxury on my final mission. Once this was done, I'd be free of the dragon forever.

Bunching the skirt, I threw it over my head and pulled. And *pulled*. How many layers did this damn thing have? It'd felt light while I was running, but perhaps that was just excitement flooding through my veins. The dragon thrashed against my ribcage, making my task no easier.

And now my arms were stuck. I gritted my teeth and swore, yanking despite the discomfort. I couldn't see, and the prince's voice was getting louder. Closer.

My petty desire was proving to be a fatal mistake.

The fabric gave way at long last. My shoulders popped free, and my arms soon followed. As the dress floated to the ground and the prince's silhouette became visible through the mist, my dragon came alive.

The act of shifting wasn't as painful as it was cathartic. Talons were first to sprout, bursting through the ends of my fingers and toes with such violence that splatters of crimson flecked the ground. Though the still-human part of me wanted to scream, I bit my tongue. The same moment hair retreated into my scalp, wings burst from my spine, and this time I couldn't stifle the guttural shriek that tore from my throat. Bones twisted, popped and snapped, and through my blurring vision, the world shrank until even the tallest oaks became little more than twigs. The pain subsided, and my sight went from hazy to razor-focused. I pinpointed the prince chasing after me. I heard his elevated heart rate clear as a war drum. I smelled his exhilaration turned to fear the moment he glimpsed me.

I yearned next to taste his blood.

He staggered backward, and a draconian laugh quaked the ground beneath our feet. The beast took over when he started to run. Snarling, I stepped forward to crush a handful of trees. Trunks and other carnage fell in his path, and he screamed before darting to find an exit.

There was one thing I loathed about this body; it was cumbersome. I could fight and kill in each of my forms, but the beast better concealed my identity, and when the dragon took over, things like emotion never got in the way. The dragon yearned for blood; nothing more, and nothing less. The human in me, no matter how much I tried to shut her out, *felt* things...so I needed to make this quick.

The sooner this ended, the better for all involved. Once I finished him, I could go home for good. Ten princes, ten kills, and I would never be tormented by the dragon again. That was the deal Rothbart and I had made...well, most of it. There was still the matter of my master's other demands, but the dragon shoved those thoughts aside.

I had a prince to devour.

He spotted the exit. The *one* exit among the trees I'd felled. *Dammit.* I smashed a log, splintering wood everywhere, but gods was he fast. Debris clouded the air, but he sprinted on, all traces of clumsiness gone as he gained ground faster than any prince I'd fought before.

I turned to the side, aware of where he stood. I could crush him, but that was no fun; the dragon preferred bones snapping and crunching beneath her teeth. Utilizing the momentum from my behemoth body, I swung my tail in a continuing arc, taking with it nearly all the trees covering the hillside and starting an avalanche of rolling trunks. The only place left to run was straight into my clutches.

But he surprised me yet again.

With nimble grace I wish I possessed, the prince faced the danger head-on. He leaped and dodged, and by some miracle made it to an outcropping of rock seconds before he'd have been crushed by a wayward boulder. He wedged himself beneath the stone, using the shield that protected him from the relentless waves of debris.

Clever as it was, it certainly wouldn't protect him from *me*.

I lowered my maw to the ground, waiting for the avalanche to subside before timing my strike. Our eyes met, and for reasons the dragon didn't understand, my heart skipped a beat. He was pleading.

He was afraid.

I wanted to scream. Didn't he know I was too? Didn't he know I was doing this to set myself free from one torment only to be immediately enslaved by another?

He was a prince. He'd never known torment a day in his life—save for what I was about to do.

I bared my teeth. His hand shot to the pommel of his sword, enraging the dragon and bringing our conjoined minds to a state in which I had little control. The rubble slowed, and though I preferred to wait before lashing out, the blade changed things. I shot forward, teeth grazing stone and earth in their search for flesh and widened my maw just enough to fit him inside.

I'd misjudged. A feral screech tore from my throat when my snout scraped the jagged surface of his shelter, and as I recoiled, blood rained down around us. The outcropping's narrow opening *had* been enough to keep me out, and my overconfidence now meant I was wounded.

The dragon's rage built to dangerous levels. My eyes narrowed into slits and my claws dug into the earth. The prince drew his sword in preparation for my strike, but when our eyes met, his gaze trailed over the blood coating my snout.

I growled. It would be *his* soon.

The prince began waving his arms like a madman. With his sword still in his hand, the blade clanged against the rock shielding him from me, and even my human half was confused. Was this a challenge? A threat? The desperation of a man who knew he was about to die?

A sword answered my question.

With another deafening shriek, I turned away from the prince and towards the forest. A company of men stood at the ready, weapons poised to strike while crests bearing the prince's colors flapped in the breeze. Turning my head back towards where he'd been trapped, I saw nothing but a wall of rock.

He'd escaped.

Their mission accomplished, a few of the men took off while the rest stood firm, banging their swords against their shields and yelling unintelligible nonsense. Cowards and fools respectively. If they thought they'd saved their beloved prince, they were sorely mistaken.

I'd kill them all.

I lunged forward. One man crunched beneath my foot while I snatched another in my jaws, his armor doing less than nothing to protect him. Before I spat him out, I went for another, relishing the sensation of bones snapping as much as I relished their screams.

I made quick work of the fools who thought they could face me, knowing the cowards who fled already had a head start. Wings beating to help propel me forward, I stomped through the trees, eyes darting in every direction to scan for movement.

There.

A straggler screamed in vain for the companions all too eager to leave him behind. As I'd done with the others, I snatched him in my claws—but this time, I didn't crush him. My taste for blood had been sated for the moment, and with a handful of victims remaining, I could have some fun.

I lifted him to my face, wanting him to feel my breath. I wanted him to see the blood of his companions staining my teeth as I bared them.

Most of all, I wanted him to scream.

He thrashed within my claws serving as a cage, suspended too high to jump. I pierced a claw into each of his feet, ignoring his howls of agony.

When he met my gaze, I tore him in half.

Blood oozed down my legs as I tossed the pieces to the dirt, already on the hunt for those that remained. My speed wasn't impressive, but my size meant each stride spanned a hundred yards. It wasn't long before another straggler fell behind; badly limping, he soon collapsed altogether. I pinpointed his location, intending to crush him as I continued my chase.

But the prince turned around.

He sprinted for his fallen man, reaching the straggler before I did, but there was no time to escape. Their only choice was to face death as one.

Instead, the prince faced *me*.

Siegfried.

Shock rippled through me at the remembrance of his name, and I skidded to a halt. Trees quivered, and even the men stilled as they watched what I would do to their prince.

Raising his sword, Siegfried screamed words the human part of me understood. "It's me you want, yes?" Without waiting for me to respond, he headed toward the lake. He may not have explained himself to his men, but his message to me was clear.

Don't harm them.

I growled. What right did *he* have to tell *me* what I should and shouldn't do? I could crush them all—especially with the way they stared at me now as if their prince's supposed sacrifice rendered them immune. I should slaughter them out of spite.

No. What little was left of my humanity forced its way to the forefront of my mind. *He's the last one—the last prince. After this, no more.*

No more.

I started after him.

Siegfried kept his breakneck pace. The closer we drew to the lake, the wetter the ground became, and the harder it was for me to slog through. I beat my wings to no avail, screeching into the color-changing sky that reminded me I didn't have much time. As soon as the sun began to rise, the dragon would leave me, and my hunt would start over. Every fiber of my being demanded Siegfried's blood, and not because I'd been ordered to end him. It was because he'd made a fool of me *and* my master. If Rothbart knew I spared those men, he'd chain me in the dungeon for at least a week—most likely more. *Best make sure he* doesn't *find out,* the human in me chastised, but keeping *anything* from the sorcerer was much easier said than done.

Cliffs lined the lake's eastern shores, offering Siegfried nowhere left to run. He gripped his sword tighter the more my shape shrouded him in shadow. *Shadow?* The sun peeked over the horizon, evaporating any traces of darkness.

I had only minutes.

Wary and afraid, he stared at me like a caged animal. If only he knew just how much I could relate.

"Did you kill her, too?"

I narrowed my gaze.

"You did, didn't you?" Siegfried's shoulders relaxed the longer he studied me. It was nearly as puzzling as the way he'd leaped to the defense of the men meant to be doing that for him. "She was just a *girl.*"

He had no idea he was talking about me.

"We knew you'd come for me. We didn't know when, but knew it would be eventually." Siegfried tossed his sword at my feet. "You sure as hell took your time."

Sunrise drew closer with every word he spoke, but I couldn't bring myself to do what needed to be done.

"I also knew I stood no chance of killing you."

I rumbled; it was true. Perhaps as a human, but never as a dragon.

"You understand every word I'm saying, don't you?"

He did it again—held me captive with his eyes. Unlike the rest of him, they were light.

Siegfried reached to unfasten his cloak. "Then understand this. I may not be able to kill you…but I *can* ensure you're not what kills me."

He jumped.

A strangled cry tore from my throat. I stumbled, belly striking stone while my neck dangled over the edge of the cliff. The lake sparkled below, reminding me it was too high a height for a human to survive the landing.

But not a dragon.

I dove after him.

The first rays of dawn licked at my scales like fire, melting them where it touched. Human skin began to surface and my limbs started to flail, no longer recognizing my mind as the entity in control. I kept my eyes on Siegfried, beating my wings before they were sucked back into my body. Ignoring the pain that shot up my arm, I reached for him. We clasped hands—*human* hands—and though mine were slick with blood, I refused to let him go.

Somewhere between forms, I pulled him against my chest, fighting against the curse harder than ever before. My wingbeats grew further apart, and with Siegfried's added weight, we were falling much too fast.

Even for the dragon.

I struck the lake first and hardest. Blinded by the pain, Siegfried slipped from my grasp and into the depths below. I couldn't even scream.

I could only surrender.

I opened my eyes expecting darkness, but instead, I saw *him*. Siegfried floated lifelessly in the lake. Eyes closed, his arms were spread wide in surrender, and nothing but peace was written all over his face. A chill that had nothing to do with the cold shot down my spine. My body screamed for the surface, but I swam toward him instead.

He didn't react when I looped an arm beneath his. The water made his weight easier to handle, but not by much. Each desperate kick not only burned energy I didn't have to spare, it sent aches of pain pulsing from my ribs to my toes. I kept my gaze trained upward but seeing what I yearned for only taunted me.

When at last I sucked in a breath, I couldn't get enough. A final pull ensured Siegfried's head was above water, but all I could do was heave and sputter while my mind cleared its haze. Little by little, my memories flooded back, confirming my deepest fears.

I'd put *his* safety over my own—and he wasn't even breathing.

I transitioned from treading water to swimming like a madwoman, wondering why the fuck I even cared. I needed him dead, and he'd seen to that himself. Yanking the body was a chore, but a justifiable one; Rothbart never minded proof of my kills. I dug my heels into the muck, muttering obscenities under my breath the entire way to the shore.

Siegfried looked far worse than he had underwater. His pale skin appeared even paler, devoid of the color that gave him life, and when I brushed my hand against his cheek, it came back icy.

It was done. I was free.

But only of the dragon.

For five long years she'd plagued me. Driven from my own kingdom with no explanation as to why or how I'd been cursed,

I turned to the one man capable of helping me. Though he'd accepted me with open arms, Rothbart had a condition of his own. The magic enslaving me was old, dark, and complex, and he'd only reverse the spell if I agreed to marry him.

But first, I had to kill for him. Princes were competition, especially for someone with no viable claim to any throne. Was it vile? Were there plenty of other men who would make kinder kings? Yes—but none of those men could help me.

Save for one.

Like every curse, mine could be broken by simpler means than acquiring the aid of a sorcerer. Killing men was far easier than finding one willing to love me and *only* me. Who could love a monster—let alone a monster who'd slaughtered so many? It was like a ridiculous storybook.

But this was real life. And fucking stupid.

He coughed, and I started so badly I swore it woke the dragon.

He was *alive?*

No. Oh, no. This couldn't be happening. To kill him now, I'd have to get my hands dirty. There were plenty of options—choking, drowning, skull-bashing—but none of them clean. It had to be done. Rothbart was my only hope of reversing the curse.

Unless I could break it.

I laughed aloud and couldn't stop. I'd sooner get Odile to compliment me.

Siegfried stirred, and I bit back a scream. Rolling on his stomach, water spewed from his throat and made hideous noises that made me want to vomit right alongside him. The torrent seemed endless; perhaps I could still get away. I pictured where I could place my feet, shifted my weight, and took the first step…

He lifted his head and looked at me.

Fucking idiot. Now I *had* to kill him.

"You're naked."

I'd forgotten that I was with my dress somewhere in the forest. Crossing an arm over my chest, I seriously contemplated the skull-bashing, but his gaze hadn't wandered.

"Who are you?"

I shook my head, blindly fishing for a stone.

"I mean you no harm. I swear it." Holding my gaze, he shuffled within reach.

I knocked him in the temple with the rock—hard enough to bruise, but not enough to kill. He slumped to the side, and rather than allowing him to tumble back into the lake, I took him in my arms.

Making *me* the fucking idiot.

With his head cradled in the crook of my elbow, I studied him yet again. He had sharp, angled features, but they weren't harsh. Full lips, a strong jaw, and firm hands, yet smooth skin wherever I touched him.

Touched?

I recoiled—only for my palm to come away crimson.

Siegfried was bleeding. Retracing my caresses, it didn't take long to locate the injury's source: a jagged cut up his side. And what could be a more perfect bandage than a clean white dress?

I shook my head. Was I seriously considering *saving* him? Choking the life from him would be relatively painless, and once done, I'd be *free*.

But even when I'd believed Siegfried dead, I hadn't felt that way. An even heavier chain constricted my heart at the thought of being married to Rothbart. He'd never once taken my feelings into consideration, not even when I'd accepted the marriage as my fate and tried to get to know him. I didn't know why he wanted me and was certain the answer would disgust me. The man was selfishness personified.

What if Siegfried was the opposite? I'd never know if he bled out in front of me.

"Fuck."

We couldn't stay in the open, but I knew the perfect hiding place. It had shielded me from Rothbart on more occasions than I could count, and I even kept a few things stashed there. No clothes, but some food meant to keep, a blanket to ward off the chill, and most important, a blade.

The one thing I truly felt naked without.

I regretted knocking Siegfried unconscious about halfway to the cavern, but the injuries I'd sustained—a stab to my rear, and bruising from the fall—were slowing me down even more than his weight. I slung his arms around my neck and bore his weight on my back, but it could only work for so long. The strength granted to me by the dragon was waning fast. Sweat pooled at my brow and I gritted my teeth to keep from groaning, but eventually, we made it.

We collapsed against the stone in a tangled heap. Though daylight was wasting and Rothbart would surely be searching for me by now, I allowed myself to catch my breath, relishing the coolness of the cavern floor at my back. The only condition was that I keep my eyes open; if they closed, sleep would claim me.

After propping Siegfried against the wall and draping the blanket over his still-wet form, I snatched my dagger from its hiding place and set off into the forest.

The trek that would have taken an ordinary human ages was, for me, uneventful. My injuries had started to heal thanks to Rothbart's magic, I knew exactly how to pick my way through the destruction caused by my dragon, and wasn't slowed by the large indents carved into the earth. I located the dress by scent, donned it, and started back towards the cave.

As the entrance obscured to an untrained eye came back into view, a knot began forming in my gut. Part of me hoped Siegfried had awoken and left.

But a stronger part of me yearned to see him again.

My conflicting emotions were starting to make me want to rip my hair out, but I'd save that for the dress. I hadn't gotten a good look at Siegfried's wound, but judging from the blood coating my palm, it needed bandaging. Using one hand to pull back the curtain of foliage, I rested the other on my brow to help my eyes adjust to the darkness.

He was awake.

And he'd removed his shirt.

Our eyes met. Siegfried leaned against the cavern wall, crimson seeping through his fingers. It appeared I'd interrupted his search for supplies.

I gestured for him to sit, and thankfully, he obeyed.

I didn't approach right away. We needed a fire. Siegfried watched as I fed logs into the makeshift fireplace; nothing more than a natural indent in the cave wall I'd used for the purpose. As I prepared to strike flint, his voice startled me.

"You, ah…live here?"

He either didn't remember or hadn't been paying attention to my hair. Not many sported ashen locks in these parts.

I didn't answer even once the fire was a decent size. I crossed to the opposite wall, reaching behind a crevice for the pail that collected rainwater seeping through a hole in the ceiling.

"Do you speak common? Can you understand me?"

I shot a glare in his direction informing him that, unfortunately, I did.

"O-okay," he stammered. "We don't have to talk—"

"You seem to be doing plenty for both of us."

He drew an audible intake of breath, eyes widening.

"What? You asked."

"I…I suppose I did." Siegfried eyed me as I settled near him with the pail. "Are you a healer?"

"Yes," I lied. "Let's see it."

He twisted to give me access to his middle. The skin was beginning to swell, framing a long slice that spanned nearly the length of his ribcage. The moment my fingers grazed its outline, a groan escaped his lips, but I could tell the wound wasn't deep. He was lucky. A good wash and bandage, and his body would do the rest.

"It's not as bad as it looks—"

"Or feels, I'd imagine," Siegfried forced through gritted teeth.

"—but I'm sure it stings like a bitch."

His head whipped in my direction.

I tore a strip of fabric from the dress I'd worked so hard to preserve. "I told you I understand common. Even the colorful bits of it."

"I misjudged you."

You don't know the half of it.

Siegfried was silent until I began tracing the now-damp rag over his injury. He tensed where I touched him, but didn't shy away. "Who are you?"

There was no harm in telling him my name. It seemed only Rothbart knew it nowadays; at his court, I was simply referred to as The Dragon.

"Odette."

"Odette," he echoed. "Does that mean white in some language?"

He may not have noticed my hair before, but he certainly noticed it now. "I've no idea." *What a strange question.*

"My name—"

"I know who you are." I lifted my gaze to his. "Prince Siegfried of Kreston."

Color sprang to his cheeks. "Was it that obvious?"

"Yes."

"I hate that," he muttered almost too quietly for me to make out—but the dragon heard everything.

"Hate what?" I was finished wiping him up, but wanting to hear his response, kept the rag pressed to his skin.

He hesitated. "That I'm always *me*."

"What's that supposed to mean?" I tightened my grip around the bloody cloth once part of my unblemished dress.

"Haven't you ever wished you could just…disappear?"

"More than you know." The words came tumbling out before I could stop them, and rage boiled beneath my skin. He *didn't* know, and he certainly didn't know me.

"Is it your hair? It's beautiful, but does stand out."

I'd been so prepared for him to question my response that when he didn't, I snapped my mouth shut.

No one had ever *not* questioned me before.

"Something like that." Too far. I'd gone too far. My insides twisted into knots in rhythm with my fluttering heart, proving my body and mind were at war. My heart knew the pain of losing.

It wouldn't a second time.

"I'm sorry," he said, startling me. "I didn't realize that was a touchy—"

"Don't be."

I worked in silence after that, bandaging his side with more strips torn from my dress. It was monotonous work: a blessing for my hands, but a curse for my mind. *Don't look,* I chastised myself each time my fingers strayed a bit too far, and each time my touch lingered too long. I refused to allow my eyes to meet his face, so they ravaged his body instead, drudging with them memories I'd worked hard to bury. *Stop it. You know better.* Heat crept to my cheeks as I secured the final knots. Nearly before I was done, Siegfried stood, all but ripping himself from my grasp.

"Thank you for your hospitality, but it's time I was on my way."

Siegfried shot out a hand to steady himself as I raised an eyebrow, unconvinced. "And where exactly would you go? Do you even know where you are?"

"It's daylight. I'm sure I could figure it out."

"You truly don't remember anything, do you?"

Siegfried scoffed. "It's…*fuzzy,* but of course I remember. I was walking in the palace gardens when I saw the most beautiful—"

He snapped his mouth shut; eyes wide as he stared at me. "Y-you—"

"*I* saved your life." I pursed my lips and tensed, preparing for a fight. "The dragon was sent to kill you—"

"No *fucking* shit!"

I held my breath, mentally picturing where I'd placed my dagger.

Siegfried's expression softened. "Odette, I didn't mean to frighten you—"

"*You* should be frightened of *me.*" I dove to the other side of the cavern, curling my fingers around my blade's hilt and holding it aloft. My eyes burned, and silently, I challenged him to come closer. *Just give me an excuse.*

I might complete this mission yet.

He could have walked away. He could have turned tail and *ran*—any intelligent man would have. Instead, he stared at me. Studying me.

"Don't pity me," I spat, trying to ignore my shaking arms.

"Who did this to you? The dragon?"

"You could say that."

Siegfried's eyes narrowed. "You work for him?"

"Her," I corrected.

"And you went against her orders—orders you've taken before. You saved *me* over all the others she's killed. Why?"

He pressed too hard and too fast. I refused to lower my knife as I held his gaze, unable to force the answer from my unwilling throat.

"How many princes have there been before me? I know of Fredrik, Stefan, Philip—"

"Stop it—"

"Why me?" he demanded. "Why the last?"

'I thought you could love me' couldn't be uttered, so I settled for the next best thing. "You're different," I blurted out. "It's because you were different."

"Different?"

"Are you always going to repeat everything I say?" I lowered my weapon but did nothing else to indicate an invitation. "Your men. You'd have sacrificed yourself for them."

"And that was *different?*"

"None of the others did it. They all died like cowards, but not before trying in vain to save their own skins."

Siegfried shook his head. "That's a ruler's job—never ask your people to do anything you wouldn't do yourself."

I laughed darkly. "Sounds like you'd have actually made a decent one. Too bad you'll never get that chance."

"What do you mean?"

"You can never return to Kreston. Not if you wish to live."

He scoffed. "I can't just abandon—"

"You can and you must," I snarled, closing the distance between us with a few practiced strides. Once we breathed the same air, I pressed the dagger to his unflinching throat. Our eyes met, and I was impressed by the fire I saw within. He was every bit as brave as he preached.

"You *can* refuse." I pressed until the tiniest bead of his blood coated my blade. "But if you do, I'll kill you here and now."

As I should have from the start.

Nothing prevented Siegfried from backing away. I hadn't shoved him against the wall. The man was unarmed. *Very* unarmed, as I was all too aware. My front pressed against his bare chest as it was the only way I could reach his neck, and it felt nicer than I wanted to admit.

Stop it.

Siegfried glared at me with enough venom to make it clear my growing desire was one-sided. He huffed in my face, gaze narrowing into slits. "You're bluffing."

Gods, even his *breath* smelled sweet. "I'd think twice about questioning the woman holding a knife to your throat."

"You didn't kill me last night. You didn't leave me to drown. And you did the *opposite* of killing me not even five minutes ago."

I stood on the tips of my toes, twisting the knife at a careful angle. "You're right—I *don't* want to kill you. But that doesn't mean I'm not changing my mind with each word you speak."

He ripped his neck away and snatched my upper arms in the same fluid motion. Before I had a chance to lash out with the blade, Siegfried twisted me around so my back pressed to him, my own head barely reaching his chin. Locking his arms around me with one hand controlling the knife, he squeezed, assuring himself he had me.

He didn't, but I certainly didn't want him knowing that. Not yet.

"And I don't want to hurt you," he whispered in my ear. "But you're right—returning to Kreston is suicide. Which is why *you're* going to help me kill the dragon."

I laughed. And *laughed.*

Siegfried's grip loosened enough for me to breathe through my hysterics. My voice echoed off the cavern walls, the volume of it hurting my sensitive ears, but I couldn't bring myself to stop for a long while.

"What in God's name is so funny?"

I couldn't answer and struggled to draw a deep enough breath. The hold around me loosened, including the hand meant to control my knife.

"Are you all right—"

"Are you certain you didn't hit your head when you fell into that lake?" I glanced over my shoulder and whipped him in the face with a sheet of white hair. "How the *fuck* do you expect to kill a beast of such behemoth proportions? *You?* A man?"

"I don't," Siegfried growled. "Not without your help."

I ripped my arm from his grasp and jabbed my elbow into his nose, feeling cartilage crunch beneath bone. As he staggered back, I whirled around, once again gaining the upper hand. Blood seeped through Siegfried's fingers and poured from his nose, and as disappointing as it was to have marred such a beautiful face, I didn't feel the least bit sorry.

"*First* of all," I snarled, "do *not* fucking touch me. And second, I've *told* you your options. Disappear or die. And I'm beginning to care less and less if you choose the latter."

It was a while before he spoke.

"You fight well."

My jaw dropped to the floor. *You fight well.* No 'fuck you,' no 'I'll not be ordered around by a woman,' no mockery or sarcasm.

A compliment.

"You disobeyed orders. The dragon wants me dead. We both need the same thing."

I glared at him.

"*Survival.*"

"And you think *killing* the dragon is the answer?"

"I suppose you would still be loyal to the beast. *Fine.* But you cannot stop me." Siegfried turned on his heel, snatched his shirt from where he'd shed it, and started for the mouth of the cavern.

Rage swelled within me. "And where do you think you're going?"

"To find someone who *will* help me." He turned around so I could hear him, walking backwards toward the exit.

"You *fucking* idiot," I spat, but he didn't slow.

"You may be content to hide, Odette, but I'm not—*what in God's name are you doing?*"

Siegfried froze the moment he noticed me holding the dagger to my wrist, eyes wide with horror.

He didn't have to be afraid. Death didn't scare me—not nearly as much as living sometimes did.

Siegfried swallowed. "Odette, *please*—"

"If you kill the dragon…you kill *me*. If that is your choice, I'll save you the trouble."

And your life.

"You don't have to do this." He took a tentative step forward, but my response was to dig the blade in till it tasted blood. The sting was intoxicating.

"Yes. I do."

"Do you mean this literally? The dragon's life is linked to yours?"

To keep from saying too much, I nodded.

"I didn't know. Please, don't do this. We'll find another way."

"*We?*" I scoffed. "You were in this for yourself just a moment ago."

"That's not fair and you know it. If the dragon can't be killed, you must know *some* way to defeat it."

"There is no way."

"Odette—"

"Will you stop saying my name? I regret telling it to you."

"I don't regret knowing it."

A chill shot up my spine. "Why?" I whispered.

Siegfried gestured toward my arm. "Put down the knife and we'll talk."

Trembling and with monumental effort, I let the blade clatter to the floor. My knees gave out, but before I collapsed Siegfried was at my side. He took me in his arms, and we sank to the floor as one, a tangled heap of limbs and blood.

"I can put you down if—"

"Stay," I ordered.

He did.

I waited for my heartbeat to settle before speaking, relishing the sensation of something so real surrounding me. I didn't enjoy being touched…but right now, it wasn't so bad.

"Love," I eventually uttered.

"Love?"

"To defeat the dragon, she has to be loved."

He was quiet for a while as I focused on steadying my breathing. At some point, he began running his fingers through my hair, and the act was so comforting, I had to fight to stay awake.

"You're certain this is the way?"

My eyes fluttered open. I shifted so I could look at his face, and before I knew what I was doing, trailed my fingers along the nose I'd bloodied. "You cannot kill a monster, so you must *love* her instead—her and no other. Whoever cursed her knows it is impossible, as well as laughable."

Siegfried winced, and I wasn't sure if it was due to my words or my touch.

"Let me clean you up—"

"No. You need to rest."

I made a feeble attempt to sit up, ignoring the rush of dizziness and nausea. "I'm fine."

"And I'm a unicorn. *Sit*, please, and stay put."

He propped me against the wall, and I watched as he fetched my rag and bucket. Once he'd wiped the blood from his face and yanked his shirt back over his head, he settled opposite me, eyeing me in a way that made me want to sock him in the mouth all over again.

"I said I'm *fine*—"

"You don't have to do this, you know. Not with me."

"Why are you still here?"

"Do you want me to go?"

My silence was enough to betray me.

"Then I'm yours, at least until you're feeling better, but I hope to be much longer than that."

Heat crept to my cheeks. "What do you mean?"

"I'm hoping you're willing to help set *both* of us free. If I'm to love this dragon, as you say…who better to teach me how?"

"Her, and no other," I reminded him. "No more chasing pretty girls at court, and no following through on whatever marriage was arranged for you. You're prepared for that?"

"Of course."

"Forever?"

"Far longer than forever."

I blinked. "You're a fool."

"Perhaps. But for the record…the only pretty girl I ever chased was you."

Dammit—he was too good at this. To keep from blushing yet again, I stole a glance at the encroaching shadows near the mouth of the cavern. It was barely midday, and Siegfried was right—I needed rest before nightfall, and Rothbart was sure to be on the prowl. I was in no condition to face him now, and especially not one to lie to him. I needed food, sleep, and a clear head.

I nodded towards the knife. "That's probably safer in your hands."

"I can't say I disagree."

"Just keep watch, will you?"

Siegfried frowned. "But the dragon only hunts at night."

"There exist monsters *far* worse than dragons."

I was too comfortable.

An arm draped lazily over my hips, fingers barely grazing stone. Steady breaths struck the nape of my neck, flooding me with warmth, and when I lifted my head, the glimmer of a knife flickered in Siegfried's opposite hand.

Keep watch, my ass.

I pushed his arm from me and then myself into a sitting position, fully prepared to give him a piece of my mind until I turned to look at him.

Siegfried's bunched-up cloak supported his head while the rest of him remained the perfect shape to fit my body, arms splayed to welcome me back if I wished. Dark, unruly locks framed closed eyes—hair I longed to twirl between my fingers—while pale skin reflected the light of the setting sun.

Curling my hand around his, I pulled the dagger from his grip.

And then I ran.

The dragon began suffocating me before I made it far from the cavern. She writhed against her internal cage, but I fought back. The sun still hung low in the sky, a palpable reminder of how little time I had left as a human, but fuck if I wasn't determined to milk every second that I could.

I stumbled through the forest with less grace than usual. My feet slid through the piles of leaves and debris, threatening to rip my legs out from under me, but I managed to grip the trees for support. Glancing through the gaps in the foliage, I gritted my teeth at the way the setting sun reflected on the surface of the lake. Brilliant reds and oranges and even some lush pink formed a breathtaking palette of wonder, colors mixing to form a natural watercolor portrait reflecting the sky.

To me, it looked like shit.

The first stabbing pain in my gut sent me doubling over. I groaned and clutched my chest, and it took effort for the sound not to turn to an animalistic snarl. Worry settled in my core. The dragon knew I disobeyed orders, and this was only the beginning of her punishment.

I made my way through the woods by instinct rather than conscious effort, unwillingly headed towards the opposite bank. There was a small inlet there; the one place where I could stand in the shallow waters as a dragon, and simply by touching me, Rothbart could return me to my human form. I tasted his scent in the air and knew he was close.

And I knew he'd require an explanation for my absence.

A *convincing* one.

When the dragon's second warning hit, I was more prepared, and gripping the dagger tighter helped to brace myself. I yearned to sink it into flesh if only to watch something other than myself bleed and in response, my arm lashed out of its own accord. The blade buried itself into a nearby tree, and though it was only sap that oozed from its wound, it was still oddly satisfying.

"Odette!"

I dropped into a crouch, breath hitching in my throat. The initial panic turned to rage, especially since the voice that called for me wasn't Rothbart.

It was Siegfried.

He tore through the forest resembling a drunken newborn

moose. He flailed his arms wildly, more than once getting his sleeves caught on branches, and continued calling for me like an idiot.

A fucking idiot.

I yanked the knife from the tree, grimacing when my fingers became coated in sap from the blade. "Do you *actually* have a death wish?"

Siegfried didn't slow. "We were supposed to work *together*!"

"Plans change."

"Mine didn't," he called breathlessly, doubling over less than thirty yards out. "Please, don't do this—"

"We've had this conversation before. I listened then—but I cannot now."

"You *can*, you just won't," he hissed through gritted teeth.

I squared my shoulders before the dragon dug her claws into my gut. Sputtering as I fought to keep her contained, a thin line of blood trailed from my lips.

"You're right."

I hurled the dagger in his direction.

I didn't wait to see whether or not the blade found its mark before I sprinted deeper into the forest. I hadn't thrown to kill— only to shock Siegfried long enough to put ample distance between us. Once shifted it would be all over, and he couldn't bear witness to my transformation.

Not if he had any chance of remaining alive.

I didn't make it far before he called for me yet again, his voice fueling my strides. I shrieked when talons came bursting through my extremities. I yanked on my hair as it disappeared back into my scalp, digging instead into my flesh when wings ripped free of their cage. My dress constricted me for only a moment before the dragon's immense form tore it to pieces, shredding with it any lingering traces of my humanity.

When I lifted my head, I saw the world through the dragon's eyes.

At the sight of me, Siegfried halted in his tracks, stumbling backward until he fell on his ass. I lowered my neck and roared in his face.

He ran.

The pull to Rothbart was strong now that I'd assumed the dragon's form. Shapeshifters were drawn to other shapeshifters, evidenced by the way I was already headed towards our spot. I was happy to let the dragon take over; the sooner we left this cursed lake, the safer Siegfried would be.

It wasn't more than a dozen strides to the inlet. I skirted around the lakeshore, careful with where I placed my feet and tail, and tasting the air for signs of Rothbart. He was close, but I hadn't yet seen him. I snorted. Fucking bastard wanted to make me wait.

Such was his game. He wanted me to *need* him.

When I stepped into the water, I was cold. A longing to be back in the cavern burned within my chest—the fire, the warmth, *Siegfried*—but I swallowed the desire. There could be no more of that where I was going. I sat on my haunches, curled my tail around my feet, and waited.

Rothbart took his damn time. Even as darkness fell, a deeper one enveloped my psyche, digging in its roots until it became difficult to draw breath. I flicked my eyes in every direction, but there was only the breeze whispering to the trees.

Hello, my swan.

I flinched at his voice in my head.

You're not happy to see me?

I can't see you, I shot back.

You simply forget where to look.

Through a gap in the foliage emerged a solid black owl. Piercing amber eyes bored a hole through me as the creature landed on the bank, but it was already beginning to transform. Wings turned to arms and talons turned to feet without any of the blood or agony my dragon demanded, possessing an unearthly grace instead. Rothbart's human appearance was rather bird-like to begin with, given his hooked nose and sunken eyes, but his more unattractive features were concealed by the facial hair he kept gruff to hide it. He knelt until the shift was complete, lifting only his head once it was done and curling his lips into a sinister smile.

"I've missed you, Odette."

I couldn't say the same.

A fully clothed Rothbart stood, black cloak billowing around his hunched shoulders. His shifts never rendered him naked, which he said was yet another result of the curse I couldn't wait to be broken. I pranced, eager for him to touch me, but he shook his head.

"Not so fast, my swan. You must tell me why you did not

return to me immediately. You know I don't like to be kept waiting."

I answered inside his head. *I got cold feet.*

"There's no need for that. We agreed to only wed once you were ready."

I would *never* be ready, and he knew it. I bit back the growl that formed in my throat, allowing silence to linger instead.

Rothbart clapped his hands. "Well, you're here now, and that's all that matters. Prince Siegfried was an easy target, I imagine?"

I nodded stiffly.

"*Details*, Odette. You know I like hearing the details."

We can discuss once I'm human.

Rothbart's head snapped up. "What did you say?"

I only meant that I've spent an additional day in the wilderness. I'm exhausted and famished, and eager to return to your fortress—

"*Our* fortress, my swan."

—so that I may rest. I bowed my head so low it nearly touched the surface of the water.

Rothbart clicked his tongue. "I do not doubt that you are exhausted, but you would not be had you returned to me when you were meant to."

He wanted me to fucking grovel. Fine, so long as we got out of this damned forest—and away from Siegfried—as quickly as possible. *I apologize, master. I was foolish and I see that now.*

"You're lucky to have such a forgiving master."

I stifled another growl. *Yes, I most certainly am.*

"In addition to being forgiving, I am also generous." He removed one of his gloves. "You need your rest more than you realize. At sunset tomorrow, we announce our engagement to the court."

I was so focused on him changing me back that I didn't register his words right away.

"I'll need you bright and beautiful," he continued, "but then again, you always are."

Before I could respond, he pressed his palm to my hide.

Water surged around me, entangling my limbs in glowing aquatic ribbons. There was no blood or pain as the world around me shrank. I continued sinking until I was a head shorter than Rothbart and regained my balance on two legs instead of four. When the waters settled, I raised my hands to my face, flexing my fingers to confirm the transformation.

Rothbart draped his cloak over my shoulders, but not before roving his eyes over my naked form. From behind, he trailed a hand down my arm.

"Better?" he whispered in my ear.

"Much," I forced, yanking the cloak so tightly it threatened to suffocate me. It didn't stop Rothbart from brushing hair from my shoulder, exposing my neck. *Don't you fucking dare*, I thought bitterly, but before he could press his lips to my skin, the snapping of a twig turned both our attentions to the forest.

Siegfried peered through the trees. And judging from the way his mouth hung agape, he'd seen everything.

Fucking idiot.

Rothbart reacted fast, but I reacted faster. Seizing the hand that had assaulted me on more occasions than I could count, I sank my teeth into flesh with no intention of letting go. As Rothbart howled and blood dripped down my chin, my eyes met Siegfried's, communicating only one thing.

Run.

Even when Rothbart began beating against my skull, I didn't release him. I clung to the obscenities that spewed from his lips, happy to wear each as a badge of honor.

"You lying, scheming *bitch*! Fucking *whore*, I'll see to it you're *never free again*!"

He ripped himself free, but not without tearing away a chunk of flesh in the process. I spat out the blood and muscle that filled my mouth, fighting to stay both conscious and on my feet.

I managed neither once the final blow found its mark.

More fucking water.

I couldn't escape it no matter how I thrashed or twisted. The icy torrent soaked me to the bone and didn't cease even when I begged. I continued screaming despite my mouth filling with the hellish liquid, and at a certain point, allowed it to make its way uninhibited down my throat.

Better to drown than be this fucking cold.

When breathing became difficult, the torrent ceased. I took a heaving breath and blinked in the darkness.

Rothbart sank to my level as I was unable to rise. My arms were extended to their full length, chains securing my wrists to each wall. My skull throbbed as if I'd been beaten, and the metallic taste of blood lingered in my mouth.

I lunged at Rothbart. "You *bastard*—"

"I'd save my strength if I were you."

"What did you do with him?" I demanded, ignoring the chattering of my teeth.

"You're not concerned with your current predicament? Interesting."

I yanked on the chains. "I've had worse—as have you. How's the hand?"

Rothbart pulled his bandaged palm closer to his chest as rage flickered in his eyes. "I underestimated how desperately you would cling to your humanity even after murdering so many."

"I'll ask again," I hissed through gritted teeth. "What have you done to Siegfried?"

"A *murderer*, Odette. That's what you are."

"For *fuck's* sake—"

"The bigger question is what you *didn't* do." Rothbart began to pace. "He was meant to be your last kill. Why throw it all away now?"

Because I fucking hate you. I bit my tongue on the off-chance Siegfried was still alive.

Rothbart halted and yanked my chin to face him. "Choose

your next words carefully, my swan."

I fought the urge to tear myself from his grip. "He escaped and I didn't feel like tracking him down."

"*LIES!*" Rothbart slapped me across the face.

I slumped forward as stars danced in my vision.

"You will tell me why you spared him, or he dies here and now."

"He's alive?" I breathed, raising my gaze to Rothbart.

The cruel smirk that spread across his features answered both our questions. "My little swan, I do think you're in *love*."

"I am incapable of love."

"Are you, now?" Rothbart gripped a rope dangling from the ceiling. "Then surely *this* won't bother you."

Something came tumbling from above. It struck the ground with a dull thud, and only once I'd gotten a good look did I shriek.

A corpse clutched the dagger I'd hurled at Siegfried.

The body was charred beyond recognition, but the dagger was proof enough. A wave of nausea threatened to spill the nonexistent contents of my stomach while tears blurred my vision. I needed to draw breath, but a heavy weight settled atop my chest. I hardly noticed when Rothbart leaned in close. Even though my wrists had been rubbed raw by the chains, I thrashed, praying my dragon would emerge to shatter them.

Rothbart brushed the hair from my shoulder. "That looks an awful lot like love to me."

I turned to bite any part of him I could reach, but he wouldn't be caught off guard a second time. As Rothbart staggered back, he spat in my direction.

"A shame, really. His last words were a vow to love only you."

He'd have broken my curse.

If I couldn't speak before, I certainly couldn't now. Sobs threatened to drown and suffocate me all at once as I stared at what remained of Siegfried's body.

Rothbart tossed something at my feet. "I'll let you two catch up, but don't stay too long. The ball will go forward as planned—with one small adjustment. Can't have anyone seeing those bruises."

I glanced at what he'd thrown.

A mask.

With a snap of Rothbart's fingers, my chains came undone. I collapsed onto Siegfried's chest. The dungeon door bolted shut, leaving me alone with my rage and pain, but there was one small detail Rothbart had overlooked. My fingers curled around the dagger.

I picked myself off the floor, clutching the mask and knife.

I hoped my master was pleased with himself. I hoped that tonight, he'd be dressed in his finest garb, and stuffing his face with the finest food. I hoped Odile would be by his side to watch.

Because tonight, I would end him.

He'd given me a white dragon mask.

I traced a finger over what was meant to resemble scales, eyes flickering to where lights reflected from the chandelier. Illumination came from every direction now that the ball was in full swing, so despite my embellishment, I couldn't be certain which reflections came from me.

Rothbart hadn't spared a single expense. Surrounding me on all sides were magnificent gowns, elaborate masks, and indulgences of every sort. Couples danced and laughed without a care in the world. In the far corner, a group of musicians played a lively tune. Food, drink, and even sex awaited me if I wanted it, but I pushed it all aside, scanning the crowd for only one man.

I swear I was shedding feathers. Picking up the heavy skirt was little help, and only succeeded in getting down stuck between my fingers. If I had any say in the matter, I'd have worn something simpler and more discreet, but Rothbart had insisted.

I couldn't wait to sink the dagger strapped to my thigh into his cold, wicked heart.

He'd been avoiding me all night, and we hadn't spoken since the dungeon. Every time I got close, he'd make a swift escape, remaining close to his daughter's side. Odile eyed me from where she and her father stood in their own private box, high above my head and far out of reach—for now.

I'd figure out a way up there even if it killed me.

I was far from the only one in a mask. Rothbart's was decorated with owl feathers while Odile wore a dragon mask eerily similar to mine. It was identical in every way save for the color: black as midnight, matching both her gown and her father's cloak. Now that I'd gotten a good look at her, I realized even her hairstyle copied mine, but it came as no surprise. She'd always been the jealous type and mimicking appeared to be all the rage. Most of the other masks were fashioned after animals. Foxes, wolves, bears, and even mythical creatures waltzed the dance floor, their elaborate designs managing to conceal identities. Even the servants donned simple black and gold masks, which unlike the guests, obscured their entire faces.

I *would* need a drink to get me through this. At any moment, the music could stop, and Rothbart would announce our engagement.

And I'd want to fucking vomit.

I staggered to a table sporting glasses of wine and downed the first to come within reach. My fingers curled around the now-empty glass, nearly shattering it. No more fucking around.

It was time to kill a sorcerer.

When I glanced up at where he'd been, both Rothbart and Odile were gone. Panic replaced the determination that had been there only moments before, intensifying further when I spotted the pair at the top of the stairs. The musicians began to quiet, and all eyes turned to Odile as she began descending the elaborate staircase. From the way her gaze lit up beneath her mask, I could tell she devoured the attention the way a starving dog would a bone.

Rothbart spread his arms, and the chatter died down to silence. "Lords and ladies, and all of my esteemed guests, welcome to this night of celebration. We gather here to honor not one, but two unions, one of which will unfold right before your very eyes."

Two? I raised an eyebrow. Had Odile grown tired of fucking each of the guards in turn, and settled on a single man? I'd have sooner imagined the stars falling from the sky.

"I have news of my own, but my daughter's will come first. Who here wishes to ask for her hand?"

Surprised murmuring broke out among the crowd as Odile sank into a deep curtsy, eyes scanning the sea of faces hungrily. With the attention focused on her and whatever imbecile foolish enough to marry her, it was the perfect opportunity for me to get to Rothbart.

I pushed my way through the bodies, paying no mind to the irritated grunts and drunken curses spat in my direction. I never took my eyes from my target. Using one hand to propel myself forward, I slipped the other beneath the folds of my gown, reaching for the blade Siegfried had so graciously left me.

This is for you.

When I placed my foot upon the first stair, Rothbart clapped his hands and laughed. I froze, but he wasn't looking at me; turning, I followed his gaze.

Odile had managed to get herself a suitor.

He rose from one knee, dressed in an elaborate doublet and tight-fitting trousers. His shoulders were broad and strong, and he wore a mask adorned with raven feathers. My eyes traced the shape of his lips, and I could have sworn that I'd stared at those lips before.

I couldn't speak. I couldn't *breathe.*

Siegfried.

I was both certain it was him and certain I was hallucinating. He planted a kiss upon Odile's undeserving palm before leading her to the dance floor. Odile whispered in his ear and seeing her lips so close to his face sent a stab of physical pain piercing through my chest.

The dragon heard every word. "I knew you'd choose me."

But how?

My palms trembled as I watched them waltz to the center of the ballroom. Odile clung to him like a parasite, grinning as though she'd won the ultimate prize, and began dancing in a way that made me both envious and nauseous at the same time. They were *good,* and they looked good. Siegfried knew the steps well and maneuvered his partner through even the most complex twists and turns, and Odile danced with the grace of a swan…if swans were jealous, scheming whores.

"Beautiful, aren't they?"

Fingers locked around the elbow meant to snatch my knife. Rothbart's scent lingered over my shoulder, and before I could move, he snaked his free arm around my waist. He pulled me against him, and even through the layers of my dress, I could feel his arousal pressing into my backside.

"He looks better with her than he ever did with you, I'd wager."

"You lied to me." I yanked against his grip.

He squeezed me so hard tears sprang to my eyes. "I said

nothing of the sort. *You* were the one to assume the sorry villager I burned at the stake was him."

"But the dagger—"

"The one strapped to your leg? He made the mistake of dropping it in the forest. I simply picked it up."

My vision began to blur, and I couldn't be sure if it was the tears or the sudden fatigue that had settled in my bones. Rothbart's grip was the only thing keeping me on my feet. "He… He wouldn't—"

"He thinks Odile is you."

And Siegfried did, judging from the look in his eyes. The way he'd looked at *me* a few short hours ago.

Rothbart's beard tickled my earlobe. "And it looks as though he's about to make a certain vow…"

"*No*," I whispered.

"…blissfully unaware he's breaking another in the process. He swore to love Odette, and dances with Odile."

As the music died, Siegfried and Odile turned to us hand in hand. With Rothbart holding me immobile, I could do nothing but watch as Siegfried knelt once again.

"My Lord Rothbart, I love your daughter more than anything else in this world. You would do me an incredible honor by granting me her hand."

That look in his eyes—he *knew* something was wrong, that something was off. I opened my mouth to scream Odile's name, but Rothbart spoke faster, digging his fingernails into my skin in the process.

"You honor *me*, Prince Siegfried. I grant you my daughter's hand on one condition: that you vow to love her, and her alone, for the rest of her days."

Don't do it, I tried to scream, but a groan escaped my lips instead when Rothbart's boot came slamming down on my foot.

"I swear it upon my life."

Odile cackled, and all I could see was red.

I was vaguely aware of Rothbart's fingers tangling in my hair to drag me down the staircase. I didn't protest when he ripped the mask from my face, nor when he tossed me at Siegfried's feet.

I only came to when he whispered my name.

He cupped my face in his hands. "Odette, I didn't know. It was all a sick fucking joke. *Please*, you must believe me—"

But soon, even his pleas faded away.

I curled into a ball and drowned the rest of the world out. Siegfried, Rothbart, Odile…none of it mattered. They'd broken me. They'd won. I yearned for the darkness to take me. I didn't want to live, and yet my body refused to die. Part of me clung to this world—the part that would live forever now that Siegfried had made it so.

It wasn't difficult to channel my despair into rage.

If they wanted a fight, I'd show them a fucking dragon.

I called to her like I'd never called before. I welcomed her power, her strength, and most importantly, her bloodlust. If I was going to die, I'd take everyone in this godforsaken castle with me.

Screaming filled my ears as the beast took hold of both

body and mind. I'd taken on the dragon's complete form without shattering the roof, but the minute I stood to my full height, the stone crumpled as easily as paper. Enormous slabs of rock shattered on the dance floor, crushing dozens of guests, but plenty still remained for me to devour. Lowering my maw to the ground, I snapped my jaws, rewarded with blood. Swiping my claws and swishing my tail yielded even more victims, but it still wasn't enough.

As much fun as I was having, I couldn't move properly. My wings yearned to spread, and more than once, my scales scraped against a stubborn piece of architecture, drawing blood even as I spilled it.

"*Odette!*"

I knew that voice. Covered in dust and splattered with crimson, Siegfried had barely survived the carnage, but survive he had.

"It's me you want, yes?"

This was fucking poetic. Despite *everything*, despite the betrayal, and despite that he'd damned me to remain a dragon for all eternity, I still wanted him. I still wanted *only* him.

Siegfried sprinted down a hall I hadn't yet demolished, presumably hoping I'd chase after him.

I'd do no such thing.

Lifting my gaze to the sky, I used both my bloodstained talons and aching wings to pull myself from the wreckage. Once free, I left behind the crumbling fortress and set off towards the only place capable of bringing my heart any solace.

The lake.

Night air caressed my scales as gently as Siegfried once held me. The moment I reached the shore, I collapsed, barely clinging to consciousness. I didn't feel myself shift back into a human—but then again, I couldn't feel anything over the agony in my chest. My insides were on fire though my heart was barely beating. I clenched my now-human fist, wishing I'd kept my talons to slice my own throat and be done with it.

"*Odette!*"

Him again. Would his efforts never cease?

Siegfried wrapped his cloak around my naked form and took me in his arms. How he'd gotten here I had no idea, but a giant dragon wasn't exactly difficult to track.

"Leave me be."

"This is my fault," he whispered against me. "All my fault."

It was, but I didn't have the heart to tell him so. "You don't need to see this."

"And you don't have to die." He pulled away to stare into my eyes—a mistake on both our parts.

"I do," I whispered. "It's the curse."

That you were meant to break, not seal forever.

Siegfried gripped me tighter, tears streaming down his cheeks. "Why didn't you tell me you were the dragon?"

"Would you have believed me?"

"Stranger things have happened...such as a prince learning to love one."

I laughed, but it only succeeded in shooting pain up my side. As I spasmed, Siegfried held me tighter and steady.

"No laughing, then," he whispered.

"There's something else I'd like instead."

I fixated on that soft mouth I'd yearned to kiss since my first glimpse of it. I leaned in close—so close I felt his breaths on my cheek—and lingered there, my lips hovering in a silent question.

He answered by pressing his to mine.

Siegfried tasted of wine, blood, and sweat. We kissed long and deep, and it was impossible to discern whose tongue had slipped into whose mouth first. All I knew was that I wasn't ready when the kiss ended but pulled away when he slipped something within my grasp.

The dagger.

With my hands gripping the handle and his hands over mine, he pointed the blade toward his chest.

"Kill me."

I hesitated. Two separate urges warred within me; one that wished to see the knife plunge into his heart, and the other that wanted to toss the blade into the depths of the lake.

And the scariest part was that I had no idea which was stronger.

Ah, Odette. Indecisive as ever.

It couldn't be—but there he was. Perched high in a tree was a black owl.

Turning back to Siegfried, I peeled his fingers from the blade. "I've made my choice."

Have you, now? Rothbart cooed inside my head. *How will you do it—slit his throat? Stab his chest? Or better yet, the femoral artery. I've always* loved *watching someone bleed out.*

Neither, I thought only to myself.

He'd come here to witness a tragedy—not live one of his own. There would never be a more perfect opportunity.

I hurled the knife at Rothbart's breast.

An even worse pain constricted my chest when the dagger found its mark, twisting and yanking on my insides as if ripping them apart. Not an owl, but a human man tumbled from the tree, eyes wide with shock at what I'd done. I fought my way through my own agony just to watch the light leave his eyes.

"I've always *loved* watching someone bleed out."

And gods, was this satisfying.

Siegfried supported my back against his shoulder. "You're bleeding."

He was right. A deep crimson bled through the blue of Siegfried's cloak, mirroring what I'd done to Rothbart.

But I no longer felt any pain.

The sunrise reflected brilliant colors over the lake, featuring hues I swore I'd never seen before. Swans emerged from their nests with rows of cygnets trailing after them, and songbirds filled the air with music grander than a symphony. Nature was celebrating, as if she knew she'd never be plagued by the dragon again, and my heart swelled right along with her.

Siegfried wrapped his arms around me. Weaving his fingers

through mine, he didn't move even when I began to grow stiff and cold, and nor when I didn't answer the whispers I could no longer hear. I tried to urge him to go, but he wouldn't listen either.

Men are foolish creatures.

But perhaps this one was different.

Coming Spring 2021!

A Land of Never After

Exclusive Teaser

No one warned me the sea would smell like shit.

In all my years spent dreaming of this moment, I wasn't entirely certain what I'd been imagining—but it wasn't *this*. The docks before me were far too crowded, the noise assaulting my ears much too raucous, and the *smell*. Not shit, I realized, but death and decay, mostly from the baskets of fish left to rot in the sun.

Inwardly, I chastised myself for cursing. If such language came spilling from my lips, Mrs. Hughes would have no qualms about taking the switch to me.

But, I reminded myself, *Mrs. Hughes isn't here.*

"Shit," I muttered under my breath, and waited.

Nothing.

"Shit." Louder this time, but still no reaction from the grimy folk who shouldered past me. "Shit, shit, *shit!*"

A few raised eyebrows, but no scolding, and that was enough for the giggling to start. I'd just *cursed,* and for the first time in sixteen years, there wasn't a soul who would stop me. Who *could* stop me. Here, I could say whatever I wanted.

Here, I was *free.*

With that glorious thought front and center, I took off sprinting. Crowds parted for me as I weaved past the merchants' stands and closer to where the ships were being loaded. My heart leaped at the sight of the magnificent sails flapping lazily in the breeze, and I wondered which would become my new home. The air grew sweeter with every step, and weight I hadn't realized I was carrying melted from my shoulders despite the pack I carried. Though winding and slippery, my feet found purchase on the wooden planks, never faltering despite my constant dodging. I suppose these orphanage shoes *were* good for something besides being ugly as sin.

"Oy, *watch* it, you little wench!"

He appeared out of nowhere, and I ducked just in time—in a way. My foot caught on the ropes hanging from the crates the burly man shouldered, and my attempts to shake it off failed. I fell on my rear in a heap of soaking-wet fabric. As he glared down at me, heat crept to my cheeks.

That's one *way to make an impression.*

But then I remembered what he'd called me, and embarrassment was quickly replaced with fury. "You'll speak to me with respect, or not at all." Definitely *not* the smartest thing to say to a man whose arm weighed more than I did, but today was a fresh start.

I *refused* to let that start mean more of the same.

To my surprise, he set down the crates before offering me a hand. "Apologies, young miss—ya jus' took me by surprise."

Batting away the hand, I stood on my own, fixing my ruined dress and ducking away from his concerned gaze. My moment of defiance broken, the embarrassment had returned with a vengeance. "It's me who shouldn't have been running. I haven't been to, ah…these parts before."

Still not making a case for yourself.

Shoving my thoughts aside, I looked to the man's face to see his confusion resolve itself.

"I get it now! Didn' recognize the uniform at first."

I bit my lip; buying new clothes to replace my orphan getup should have been my first stop.

"Ya must be terribly lost. It's a long way back to the orphan—"

"I'm not going back there," I snapped too quickly. Clearing my throat, I continued, "What I mean is they won't have me. I've aged out."

The man raised an eyebrow. "You can't be a day older than—"

"I'm sixteen today." I raised my chin. "And *perfectly* capable of caring for myself."

He held up his hands in surrender. "Suit yerself, lass." With that, he began packing up his crates, and only then did I notice the inscription stamped upon each one: *Fortune's Favor*. My breath hitched; fortune certainly was in my favor today. I hadn't heard of many ships, but as the largest and grandest to ferry goods into our humble port, *everyone* knew of this one.

"*F-fortune's Favor*," I stammered. "You sail with her?"

"Aye. What's it to ya?"

"You know its Captain, then. Captain Harlow?"

"Aye." He hadn't even looked up from his work, and was nearly prepared to walk away.

I stepped in his path. "Take me to him."

This earned me another puzzled look, but this time, it was coupled with a scoff. "Aren't ya a bit small to be barkin' orders?"

"It wasn't an order—it was a request."

"Didn't sound much like one—"

"*Please*. Take me to your Captain, please."

He chuckled. "And what business does a lass have with my Captain? He's a busy man, so yeh'd best make it good."

"I'll discuss my terms with him, and him alone." I was pushing it now, I knew, but I had nothing but what I carried on my back—nothing I couldn't afford to lose.

The sailor frowned and wagged a finger. "Nice try, lassie, but I ain't playin' this game. You'll tell *me* yer terms, and then *I* decide if it's worth troublin' my Captain 'bout."

I swallowed. *Nothing left to lose*. "I…I seek employment."

There it was; my deepest desire out in the open, free as the breeze, and I could no longer take it back. I'd kept my dream of sailing the high seas to myself ever since I'd been nicknamed 'Wayward Wendy,' but it hadn't stopped the other children from laughing and making their cruel jokes.

He stared at me, blinking as though I'd spoken in tongues. "A lassie—a *deckhand?*"

I nodded. "I'll accept whatever the Captain offers. That would be a wonderful start."

"A *start?*"

"Well, yes, I don't expect I'd scrub the galleys for the rest of my days—"

"Have ya sailed before?"

I swallowed. "No."

"Have ya been *on a ship* before?"

"No, but—"

"Lass," he sighed, "ships ain't no place for—"

"A *woman* can do anything a man can." I balled my hands into fists; I hadn't come all this way to be told no by someone who'd reduce my worth down to my sex. "I can clean, I can cook, and I'm a quick learner."

"Aye, anyone *can* do such things." He shouldered his crates. "And we just happen to have *men* doin' em. Step aside."

I glowered. "No."

"Lassie, don't make me force ya—"

Force—my eyes darted to the knife sheathed at his belt. His hands were occupied.

Mine weren't.

I was shocked by my own actions and my heart threatened to beat out of my chest, but before either of us knew how, I'd turned his own knife against him. The weapon felt strange in my hands and weighed more than I expected, my hands and voice shook, but my feet were planted firm.

"I told you I learn quickly."

to be continued...

ABOUT THE AUTHOR

Raelynn Davennor has been creating and discovering fantastical worlds for as long as she can remember—often getting scolded for reading while her teachers were talking. As both an author and composer of music, Raelynn utilizes her creations in her fictional worlds full of darkness, dragons, and sassy heroines. She's made appearances with artists such as The Who, Weird Al, and Hugh Jackman, and performed on many of the largest stages in the United States. Her inspiration takes no mercy on her despite her busy schedule.

Even when completing the most mundane tasks, Raelynn is usually lost in her head, flying across the sea on the back of a dragon or humming a tune she can't wait to scribble down. In her little remaining free time, she enjoys pampering her menagerie of pets and pretending she isn't an adult.

Connect on social media!

https://www.rldavennor.com

https://www.facebook.com/groups/raelynnshorde

Facebook

Instagram

Twitter

@rldavennor

And if you enjoyed this book, don't
forget to leave a review!

www.ingramcontent.com/pod-product-compliance
Lightning Source LLC
Chambersburg PA
CBHW030755110726
47900CB00008B/2622